Sindbad

FROM THE TALES OF
THE THOUSAND AND ONE NIGHTS

Retold and Illustrated by Ludmila Zeman

Tundra Books

Published in Canada by Tundra Books, *McClelland & Stewart Young Readers*,
481 University Avenue, Toronto, Ontario M5G 2E9

Published in the United States by Tundra Books of Northern New York,
P.O. Box 1030, Plattsburgh, New York 12901

Library of Congress Catalog Number: 98-75028

Canadian Cataloguing in Publication Data

Zeman, Ludmila
    Sindbad : from the tales of The thousand and one nights

ISBN 0-88776-460-6

I. Title.

PS8599.E492S56 1999   jC813'.54   C98-931959-8
PZ8.Z45Si 1999

We acknowledge the support of the Canada Council for the Arts and the Ontario Arts Council for our publishing program.

We acknowledge the financial support of the Government of Canada through the Book Publishing Industry Development Program for our publishing activities.

Design by Sari Ginsberg

Printed and bound in Hong Kong, China

1 2 3 4 5 6   04 03 02 01 00 99

In love and gratitude, to my dad, Karl Zeman, by whose side I worked on the film Tales of a Thousand and One Nights. *His imagination and love of the story inspired me to create this book.*

Long ago there lived a cruel king. Every night he took a new wife and every day at dawn he ordered his vizier to behead the unfortunate woman. Shahrazad, a young and beautiful maiden, proudly said, "I will put an end to the king's wicked ways." She marched into the grand palace and threw herself before him. "Take me as your wife, Sire!" The king favored her beauty and they married that same day.

When night fell, Shahrazad turned to the king. "Do not go to bed, Sire, for I have a tale to tell." Rays of morning sun brushed against her satin hair when she was but halfway through. The king raised his head and whispered, "My eyes are weary; I must sleep. Finish the tale when I awake."

The king slept throughout the day. Upon nightfall Shahrazad finished her story and started another. This one was even more enticing than the first and, again, she did not reach the end by dawn.

For a thousand and one nights, Shahrazad charmed the king with her tales. He forgot his cruel ways, and ordered his craftsmen to weave the stories into the finest colored silk carpets. The elaborate patterns they made with golden threads would be admired by people around the world, and the stories would never be forgotten.

This is one of the tales that enchanted the king as it may enchant you.

It was a hot summer day in the city of Baghdad. Sindbad the Porter ached under a heavy load as he passed a handsome old man, resting in a comfortable litter. Servants waved their mighty fans, calling their master Sindbad. The poor porter looked on with weary eyes and murmured to himself: *How dare this man, with the same name as mine, have such wealth and comfort all around? How much fairness can there be when a man like him never feels the heavy load and misery that lies upon me?*

He had hardly finished his lament when one of the servants grasped his arm and whispered in his ear, "Follow me to my master's palace. He calls for you."

The porter tried to run away, fearing the powerful Sindbad, but it was too late.

The porter was led into a magnificent house filled with exquisite splendor.

"Sit down, Porter, and eat all you desire," said the old man. "I heard your lamentation outside, and you are correct. How curious it is that our names are the same, yet our state is not. But all is not as you suppose, for I, too, have known hunger, thirst, and great danger. I will tell you my story:

My father was the richest merchant in the city of Baghdad. When he died, he left me remarkable wealth and many estates. I was young then, so I took to extravagant living. I ate and drank lavishly and went about with wasteful men, thinking this way of life would last forever.

For a short time I lived without a care, but soon my wealth was gone. I lost my place to live and, curiously, all the dear 'friends' who loved me disappeared at the same time as my fortune. Alas, I was forced to sell all I had left. I boarded a ship that sailed down the river to Basrah and out to sea.

I became merely a poor sailor on a merchant ship, but I tried to learn the languages and customs of the foreign lands that we encountered. I became fond of this adventurous way of life.

One day, after a long sea voyage, we came to a small island as beautiful as the Garden of Eden.

This place where we anchored was no island, but a gigantic whale floating on the sea. Over time, sands had settled and trees had grown on the whale's back. Now she was awakened by the hiss of the fires and the jab of my saber thrust into her hide. She rose from the ocean in fury!

I became merely a poor sailor on a merchant ship, but I tried to learn the languages and customs of the foreign lands that we encountered. I became fond of this adventurous way of life.

One day, after a long sea voyage, we came to a small island as beautiful as the Garden of Eden.

Our feet had not touched the earth for months, and when the captain put out the landing planks, all the merchants rushed to shore. Some built fires and prepared elaborate dishes. Others, as curious as myself, set out to explore the island.

There were wondrous palm trees that bore hard, wooden fruit, with liquid inside. I decided to open one piece with my dagger. The wooden ball split in two, and my weapon cut deep into the ground. In my amazement, a giant stream of blood gushed into the air, and the island shrugged as if the sea was engulfing it with all its strength. The captain, who had stayed on the ship, screamed in terror: 'All aboard! Run for your lives!'

This place where we anchored was no island, but a gigantic whale floating on the sea. Over time, sands had settled and trees had grown on the whale's back. Now she was awakened by the hiss of the fires and the jab of my saber thrust into her hide. She rose from the ocean in fury!

Suddenly we were all swallowed up by the great waves. Struggling and gasping for air, I saw a wooden barrel from the ship floating above me. With my last bit of strength, I swam toward it and held on as if it were the very last friend I had.

I paddled after the ship with bare hands, but all I saw was a small shadow, disappearing in the far horizon. As darkness surrounded me, I drifted alone on my new vessel, awaiting my doom.

After many moons had passed, I caught sight of an island with a smooth white mountain. Whipped by cruel winds and bruised by merciless rain, I pressed on with renewed hope in my heart.

When I reached land, I fell into a deathlike sleep. The next morning I was woken by the sun, grateful that my life had been spared. As I lay with my eyes closed, I sensed sudden darkness fall upon me like a heavy cloak. I looked up and froze in fear. A giant bird was flying toward the island, clutching a baby elephant in its claws. Its wings were so large, they covered the entire sun.

Suddenly I realized that the mountain was the bird's egg and the island was its home. The bird covered the egg with its large, feathered body and fell asleep. I knew this giant creature must be the great Roc. When I recovered from the shock of seeing it, I decided Roc would be my means of escape. Wherever the bird would take me must be better than this desolate island!

Unwinding the turban from my head, I tied myself securely to one of Roc's talons. All night I waited, so afraid that I did not close my eyes for a moment. Only at dawn did the bird lift me into the sky.

We drifted above the ocean, through heavy fog and rain, until Roc descended into an exceedingly deep and wide valley. When we touched the ground, I quickly untied my turban and hid behind a large stone. As I looked up, all I could see in the darkness was Roc against the moonlit sky, clutching a slithering dark object. Roc's prey was a serpent whose vast length I had never before seen. The giant bird then vanished from my sight and, exhausted, I fell into a deep sleep.

I awoke paralyzed with fear. Deadly snakes and vipers surrounded me on all sides, preparing to devour me. When I looked around for help, I was blinded by a brilliant glow. I realized that these beasts were keepers of great diamonds borne out of this valley.

Suddenly a piece of raw flesh came tumbling down toward me, followed by a flock of ravenous vultures. The snakes quickly retreated into their lairs, and I began to plan my escape from this treacherous place.

I remembered a story I had heard on an island where the merchant ship once took us:

> The Valley of Diamonds is hidden between high mountains, steep and jagged. Wild beasts guard each side. Brave men, who try to climb down, never return. For many, the valley seems unreachable, but man's greed is stronger than fear. Clever merchants have found a way to bring the diamonds out of the abyss. They throw raw meat down from the highest cliffs and, as it lands, large diamonds stick to it. Hungry vultures, who circle above the valley, quickly swoop down to pick up the diamond-studded meat and carry it to their nests.

I knew that the vultures were my only hope of escape from the deadly snakes and vipers. Only they could carry me out of the valley! Unknowing of what misfortune lay ahead, I was certain that I could not live another night among the slithering beasts.

I filled my pockets with huge diamonds and waited as another piece of raw meat fell before me. In haste I tied myself to the bloody flesh and felt myself lifted into the air. The vulture slowly ascended, holding on to its prey. I knew that once in its nest, I could never escape. This wild bird would tear me apart before I could even untie myself. I prayed for a miracle to save me from this horrible end.

Suddenly the air was filled with the banging of dishes, basins, and sabers. Startled, the vulture dropped its catch, and I began to fall. I awaited my death with closed eyes when my descent was stopped abruptly by a tree branch. Opening my eyes, I saw several merchants standing before me in sheer terror. They had expected to find diamonds stuck to raw flesh, not a bloodied man who was still alive.

I extended my shaking hand, exposing the diamonds I had picked up. Their brilliant glow caused an immediate sensation. My diamonds were much greater than those that usually stuck to the raw flesh. The merchants were overjoyed when I promised them the diamonds in exchange for passage on their ship. So again I drifted on the ocean, hoping my fate would one day return me to Baghdad."

Sindbad leaned toward the porter and said, "At the time, I did not even imagine the incredible adventures still ahead. But I must rest now, my friend. Come back tomorrow and I will tell you what I endured on my next voyage."

Author's Note

The stories told by Shahrazad to King Shahriyar over a thousand and one nights have a long and complex history. The author and date of origin are uncertain since the stories were transmitted orally and compiled over several centuries. The first known reference dates back to the ninth century, to a collection of Persian tales. Other popular stories of Arabic, Indian, and European influence were gradually added over time, resulting in what is now known as the tales of *The Thousand and One Nights,* or *Arabian Nights.*

Without a doubt, the best-known stories are the adventures of Sindbad the Sailor — some of the world's most extraordinary sailing stories, which have become classics in the literature of exploration. Sindbad became an important historical figure because his travels were linked to actual voyages of the Arabs. Seven centuries before Columbus, the Arabs, who were remarkable sailors, mastered the route to China, seeking the riches of the Orient. Their route resembled that of Sindbad. They sailed on the Arabian Sea around India and Sri Lanka. In Sindbad's adventures, we visit the Valley of Diamonds, possibly the island of Sri Lanka, known for precious stones, such as rubies, blue sapphires, and topazes. Later, Sindbad is captured by manlike creatures — could they be the orangutans that Arabian sailors first encountered in Sumatra?

The mixture of fact and fiction inspired me to visually portray the adventures of Sindbad the Sailor. As an artist, I wanted to recognize Persian influence in the art of book illustration, calligraphy, layout, illumination, and border decoration. This book, created in the style of Persian script, portrays the designs and feel of the magnificent Persian carpets. To replicate their concept, I studied Persian miniatures, Oriental carpets, illustrated manuscripts, and paintings of Islamic lands in museum exhibits in London, Paris, New York, and Berlin.

Although my primary aim was to give children a sense of history, geography, and oriental cultures, I discovered that the tales of *The Thousand and One Nights* possess an even greater value. The underlying theme of all the stories is the appreciation of literature and storytelling. Elegant speech and the ability to present words cleverly was highly valued and an essential in the attainment of social status. After all, it was Shahrazad's knowledge and wit that softened King Shahriyar's cruelty and eventually defeated him.

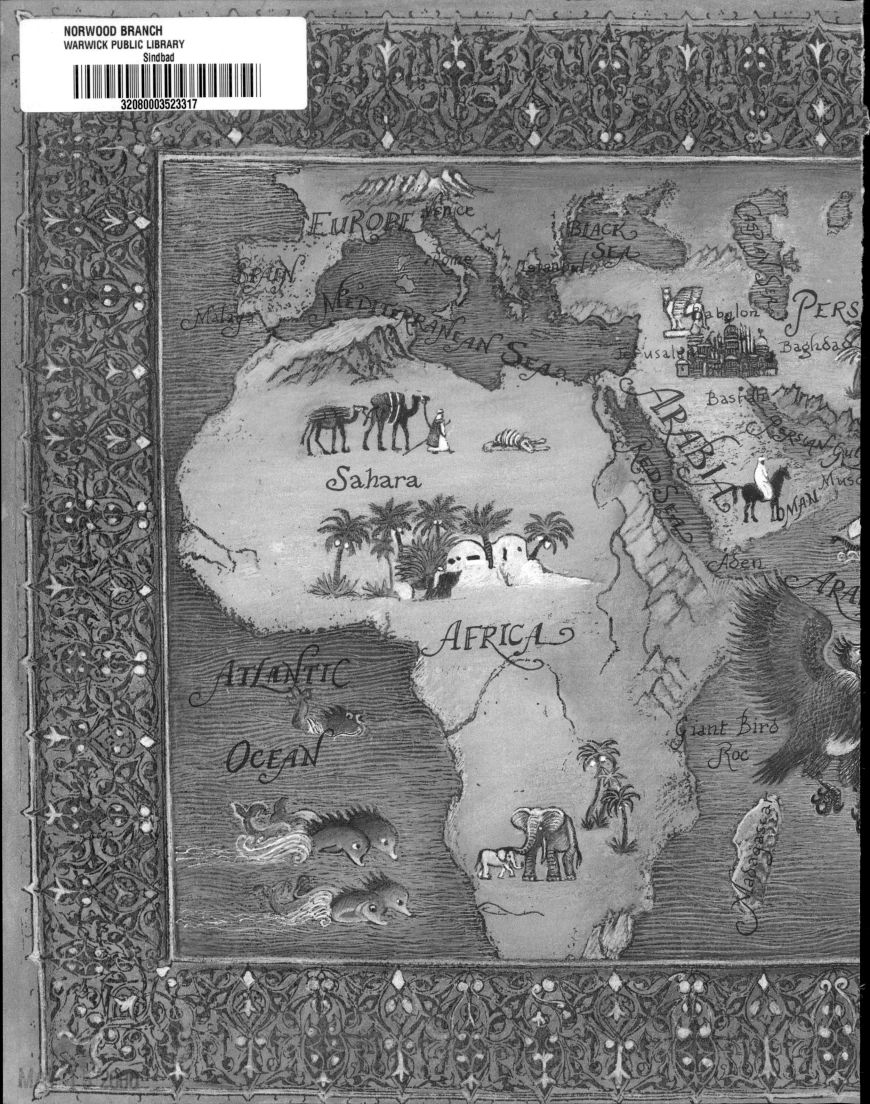